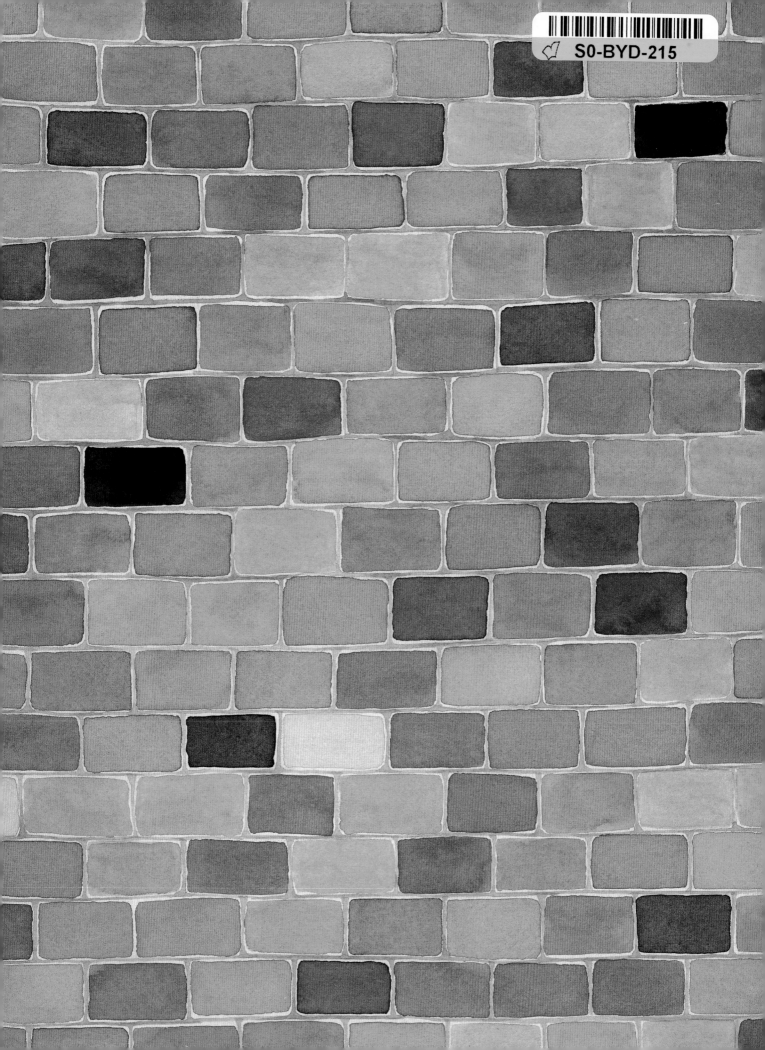

AUGUST HOUSE
Littlefolk

The Pig Who Went Home on Sunday

AN APPALACHIAN FOLKTALE

Donald Davis · Illustrated by Jennifer Mazzucco

To all the relatives who heard and loved stories and gathered to tell
them again and again . . . often on Sundays.—D.D.
To all the strong and amazing women I know—
especially my mom and sister.—J.M.

Text © 2004 by Donald Davis, Storyteller, Inc.
Illustrations 2004 © by Jennifer Mazzucco.

Published 2004 by August House LittleFolk,
P.O. Box 3223, Little Rock, Arkansas 72203
501-372-5450
http://www.augusthouse.com

Book design by Mina Greenstein
Manufactured in Korea
10 9 8 7 6 5 4 3 2 1

LIBRARY OF CONGRESS CATALOGING-IN-PUBLICATION DATA

The pig who went home on Sunday : an Appalachian folktale / Donald Davis;
illustrated by Jennifer Mazzucco.
p.   cm.
Summary: An Appalachian variant of "The Three Little Pigs," in which Mama Pig sends
her three sons out into the world with good advice that only one heeds.
ISBN 0-87483-571-2 (alk. paper)
[1.Pigs—Folklore. 2. Folklore—Appalachian Region.] I. Davis, Donald, 1944–
II. Mazzucco, Jennifer, 1972–   ill. III. Three little pigs. English. IV. Title.
PZ8.1.D289 Pi 2001
398.2'0974'04529633—dc 21
[E]   00-068937

The paper used in this publication meets the minimum requirements of the
American National Standards for Information Sciences – Permanence of Paper
for Printed Library Materials, ANSI.48-1984.

A long time ago, there lived a Mama Pig.
She had three little pigs named Tommy, Willie, and Jackie.

Day after day, these pigs ate and slept. They grew until they could not fit in their cave anymore.

One day Mama Pig called to Tommy, the oldest. "It is time for you to leave home and learn to take care of yourself." That night she picked out the things that Tommy would need when he left home.

The next morning, after breakfast, Mama Pig said to Tommy,
"Now, let me tell you two things: If you have to build a house,
build it out of rocks and bricks. And *please* come home
and see your mama on Sunday."

Mama Pig kissed Tommy on his snout and
said goodbye.

Tommy pulled his wagon down the road. He did not see the fox hiding in the bushes until it jumped right out in front of him.

"Little pig," said the fox. "Where are you going?"

"I'm going to build a house and learn to live on my own," Tommy answered.

"What are you going to use to build your house?" asked the fox.

"My mama told me to build it out of rocks and bricks," Tommy answered.

"Don't build a house out of rocks," said the fox. "A house of rocks might fall down and mash you flat. Build yourself a house out of cornstalks."

So Tommy went down the road and
built a little house out of cornstalks.

That night, as he was cooking his supper, he heard a sound: *"Gulp!"*

It was the sound of a little pig being swallowed by a fox.

And Tommy Pig did not go to visit his mama on Sunday.

Meanwhile, the other two pigs were eating and sleeping. Mama Pig called to Willie: "It is time for you to go and learn to take care of yourself." That night she packed up the things Willie would need when he left home.

The next morning Mama Pig said to Willie: "Let me tell you two things. If you have to build a house, build it out of rocks and bricks. And *please* come home to see your mama on Sunday!"

Then she kissed Willie on his snout, and he left.

It is very hard for a pig to push a wheelbarrow. Willie didn't see the fox hiding in the bushes until it jumped out in front of him.

"Little pig," said the fox. "Where are you going?"

"I'm going to build a house of my own and learn to take care of myself," answered Willie.

"Now, little pig, just in case you are thinking about building a house out of rocks and bricks, let me give you some advice. The rocks and bricks around here are too cold to make houses out of. If you want a warm house, build yourself a den in the side of a haystack."

So Willie went down the road and made a
little den right inside a haystack.

That night, as he was cooking his supper,
he heard a sound: *"Gulp!"*

It was the sound of a little pig being
swallowed by a fox.

And Willie Pig did not go to visit his mama on Sunday.

Meanwhile, back up at the cave, Jackie and his mama ate and slept. Soon Jackie said to his mama: "It is time for me to leave home and learn to take care of myself."

That night Jackie took a huge sack and loaded up the things he would need to take care of himself.

Jackie wanted to be sure he could find his way home. So as he carried his sack down the road, he looked all around him. Soon he noticed a great big, slobbery, long-toothed fox sneaking from tree to tree.

"Hello, Fox!" Jackie said.

That surprised the fox so much he nearly jumped out of his fur!

Jackie said, "I am going out into the world to learn to take care of myself and build myself a house."

Now the old fox smiled. "Folks around here don't live in houses," he said to Jackie. "They live under trees. Then they pile up some leaves to sleep on and cover themselves with more leaves."

"Thank you, Mister Fox," said Jackie. But as soon as the fox was out of sight, Jackie started picking up rocks and bricks.

Before the day was over Jackie had built himself a fine little house out of rocks and bricks.

Jackie unpacked the things from his sack. He built a fire in his stove, put on a big pot of beans, and leaned back to rest in his rocking chair.

All of a sudden he heard a loud knock on the door.

"Who is there?" Jackie called out.

"It's Mister Fox. I just came for a visit since you're going to be my neighbor."

"This isn't a good time," said Jackie. "I haven't had time to get things ready for company. You'll have to come back later."

"Oh well," said Mister Fox, "if that's the way you want to be. But it is very cold out here, little pig. Before I go on back home, wouldn't you just let me get my nose warm?"

It won't hurt just to let him get his nose warm, Jackie thought. He opened the door just a little.

When the fox jumped for the door, Jackie slammed it shut right on the fox's nose!

"How does it feel to have your nose warm?" Jackie asked.

"It feels sooooo good!" said the fox. "Now, would you let me get my head warm?"

Jackie thought about it. Then, slowly, he began to open the door.

When the fox jumped for it again, Jackie slammed the door shut right on the fox's neck!

"How does it feel to have your head warm?" Jackie asked.

The fox could hardly talk, but he croaked, "It feels sooooo good! Now, would you let me get my body warm?"

Jackie thought about it. Then, slowly, he began to open the door just a little more.

When the fox jumped for it again, Jackie slammed the door shut right on his tail! It almost cut his tail right off. He was still stuck fast in the door.

"How does it feel to have your body warm?" Jackie asked.

The fox's tail hurt more than anything in the world. Still, he said, "It feels sooooo good! Now, if you would just let me get my tail warm, I would be ready to go on back home."

Jackie wanted the fox to go back home. Slowly, he began to open the door.

As soon as Mister Fox's tail was loose, he made a jump for it. He was in the house.

Getting in the door had tired the old fox out. He stretched out beside the warm stove, and in a moment he fell asleep.

In a few minutes the fox was talking in his sleep.

"Pork and beans for my supper! Pork and beans for my supper! Yum yum yum! Pork and beans for my supper!"

Jackie looked at the pot of beans on the stove. Then he looked at himself in the mirror. All of a sudden he realized that he was the very thing the fox was planning to eat.

Jackie reached for the door, but the fox was sleeping right in front of it. He opened the shutter and looked out the window. Then he let the shutter fall with a bang.

The fox jumped up. "What was that?" he said.

Jackie smiled. "Oh, I heard something outside. I looked out to see what it was. It just turned out to be some fox hunters."

"Fox hunters! Did you say fox hunters? I am a fox, little pig! Hide me, little pig, hide me!'

Jackie looked at the butter churn his mama had sent with him. "Well, Mister Fox," he said, "I guess you can hide in here." The fox quickly climbed into the churn.

Jackie opened the door of his house. Then he rolled the butter churn out the door and down the hill.

The fox laughed because he thought he was getting away from the hunters.

But as the churn rolled away, it was Jackie Pig who laughed the most. He watched as the churn splashed into the water and floated down the river. It took the old fox so far away that Jackie would never see him again.

And that Sunday, Jackie Pig went home
to see his mama.

About the Story

My memory of the Little Pigs story is forever linked with an event that happened when I was eleven years old. The year was 1955, and our family had just gotten our first television set. We could get one snowy channel, WLOS-TV 13 in Asheville, North Carolina.

My brother and I loved to see the old black and white cartoons of Betty Boop and others (though our favorite was the Little Rascals). One Saturday our grandmother was visiting, and we were proudly showing off the new television. When we turned on our one channel, cartoons came on.

Grandmother thought Betty Boop was pretty funny. Then a cartoon came on of the story of the Three Little Pigs, which showed the little pigs escaping and then dancing around singing, "Who's afraid of the Big Bad Wolf?" When this came on, Grandmother was enraged. She made us turn the television off immediately, and she would never look at it again.

Later on, Grandmother told us why she was so upset: an important story had just been ruined. The import of the story was destroyed when the little pigs escaped the wolf and danced around and sang. She told us that this cartoon just taught children that they could do the wrong thing and still get away with it.

In all its old oral versions the pig story is a cautionary tale designed to protect children's lives by teaching hard lessons. The messages are that leaving home is dangerous, the woods are dangerous, wild animals are dangerous, and you must do what adults wisely advise in order to stay alive. (Many teachers in the city schools that I visit remark on the applicability of these precautions for the children they teach today.)

The story is ancient. In *The Grandfather Tales* Richard Chase records a version called The Old Sow and the Three Little Shoats. While sows and shoats were familiar in the world of my childhood, my grandmother always told the story in more androgynous terms. I have a feeling that my grandfather would have told it as a sow story, but, since the term *sow* was also used as a term of human derogation, Grandmother would not have told it that way.

In my visual imagination, it was always one of my favorite childhood stories.